TH
OF ROMULUS

This book has been specially written and published for World Book Day 2007.

World Book Day is a worldwide celebration of books and reading. This year marks the tenth anniversary of World Book Day in the United Kingdom and Ireland.

For further information please see www.worldbookday.com

World Book Day is made possible by generous sponsorship from National Book Tokens, participating publishers, authors and booksellers. Booksellers who accept the £1 Book Token themselves fund the full cost of redeeming it.

To find out more about the Roman Mysteries, visit www.romanmysteries.com

THE ROMAN MYSTERIES
by Caroline Lawrence

And look out for:
The First Roman Mysteries
Quiz Book *(March 2007)*

Roman Mysteries
Mini-Mysteries *(June 2007)*

The Second Roman Mysteries
Quiz Book *(July 2007)*

— A Roman Mystery —

THE CODE
OF ROMULUS

Caroline Lawrence

Orion
Children's Books

First published in Great Britain in 2007
by Orion Children's Books
a division of the Orion Publishing Group Ltd
Orion House
5 Upper St Martin's Lane
London WC2H 9EA

The Orion Publishing Group's policy is to use papers that
are natural, renewable and recyclable products and made
from wood grown in sustainable forests. The logging and
manufacturing processes are expected to conform to the
environmental regulations of the country of origin.

A catalogue record for this book is
available from the British Library

ISBN-13 978 1 84255 580 4

Typeset at The Spartan Press Ltd,
Lymington, Hants

Printed in Great Britain by
Clays Ltd,
St Ives plc

www.orionbooks.co.uk

To my brilliant editor Jon,
and the great team at Orion!

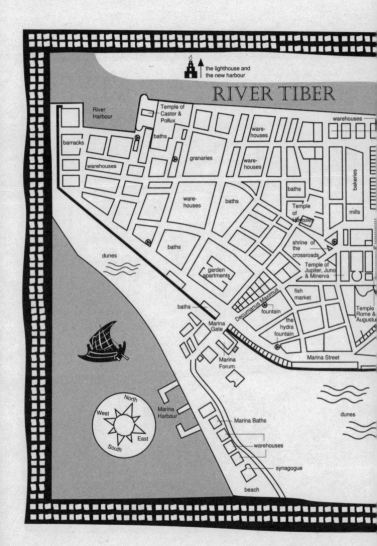

the lighthouse and
the new harbour

RIVER TIBER

River
Harbour

Temple of
Castor &
Pollux

baths

warehouses

warehouses

barracks

warehouses

granaries

warehouses

baths

bakeries

baths

ware-
houses

baths

Temple
of
Hercules

mills

shrine of
the
crossroads

dunes

baths

Temple of
Jupiter, Juno
& Minerva

garden
apartments

baths

fish
market

Temple
Rome &
Augustus

Decumanus Maximus

fountain

the
hydra
fountain

Marina
Gate

Marina Street

Marina
Forum

North

West

East

South

Marina
Harbour

Marina Baths

dunes

warehouses

synagogue

beach

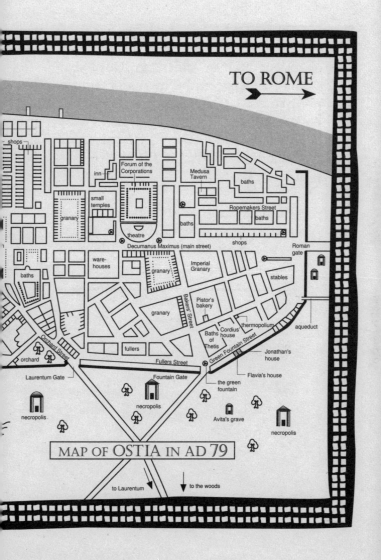

TO ROME

shops

Forum of the
Corporations

inn

Medusa
Tavern

baths

small
temples

Ropemakers Street

granary

baths

baths

theatre

Decumanus Maximus (main street)

shops

Roman
gate

ware-
houses

Imperial
Granary

granary

stables

baths

aqueduct

Bakers Street

granary

Pistor's
bakery

thermopolium

Cordius
house

Baths
of
Thetis

Green Fountain Street

Jonathan's
house

Orchard Street

fullers

Fullers Street

Flavia's house

orchard

the green
fountain

Laurentum Gate

Fountain Gate

necropolis

necropolis

Avita's grave

necropolis

MAP OF OSTIA IN AD 79

to Laurentum

to the woods

The Code of Romulus takes place in ancient Roman times, in November AD 79, between the events of Roman Mystery V, *The Dolphins of Laurentum*, and Roman Mystery VI, *The Twelve Tasks of Flavia Gemina*. Read more about these books at the end of the story.

If some of the words in the story look strange, 'Aristo's Scroll' on page 57 will tell you what they mean and how to pronounce them.

THE CODE
OF ROMULUS

'I *am* a detective!' cried Flavia Gemina, and she almost stamped her foot. 'I've solved lots and lots of mysteries!'

Because her mother was dead and her father was often away on voyages, Flavia was probably the most independent ten-year-old girl in the Roman port of Ostia.

'Detective?' Flavia's tutor Aristo raised an eyebrow. He was a good-looking young Greek with curly hair the colour of bronze. 'There's no such word in Latin. You made it up.'

'I did *not* make it up,' said Flavia. 'It was in a scroll Admiral Pliny gave me before he died. The word *tego* means "I cover", so *detegere* means "to uncover" and a *detective* is "someone who uncovers the truth".'

'Show me where it says that.'

'I can't. The scroll was lost in the eruption

I

of Vesuvius.' Flavia looked out through the columns of the peristyle into the wet green garden. She still felt a pang when she remembered the old admiral dying on the beach a few months earlier. 'It was the only scroll in existence,' she said, 'written in his own minuscule handwriting.' Flavia looked at Aristo again. 'But I remember reading that word: "detective". As soon as I saw it, I knew: I'm a detective.'

Aristo stroked his chin meditatively. 'Now that you mention it, there is a word detector. It means someone who uncovers the truth—'

'Or in my case: detectrix! Because I'm a girl.'

Aristo laughed. 'Well, being a "detectrix" or a "detective" or whatever you want to call it is no excuse for ignoring your homework. So sit down and do that calculation again the way I showed you yesterday.'

Flavia sighed and sat and stared at her abacus. But its boxwood beads were inscrutable.

Across the table, a brown-eyed boy was mouthing something at her. Jonathan ben Mordecai was Flavia's next-door neighbour and friend, as well as her classmate. He and his family were Jewish; they had escaped the destruction of Jerusalem ten years earlier and had now settled in Rome's port town. Flavia looked up at him from under her eyebrows, but she couldn't understand the words he was silently forming.

To her right, a dark-skinned girl was pointing behind her hand at one of the rows of beads. Flavia's ex-slave-girl Nubia had only been in Italia for a few months, but she was already skilled at using an abacus. Unlike Flavia.

Finally Flavia glanced at Lupus, the youngest of them. Until recently, Lupus had been a homeless beggar, but even he was better at maths than she was. Because he was mute, Lupus mainly used a wax tablet to communicate. He was casually writing something on it now and she read:

USE THE TENS COLUMN

But the words on Lupus's tablet may as well have been Etruscan. Flavia would have to admit defeat.

'I didn't do the homework,' she said in a small voice.

'Well then,' said Aristo. 'You know the punishment.'

'No!' she wailed.

'You can't object,' said Aristo. 'Last month I asked each of you to choose the punishment you thought best if you didn't do your homework. The choice was yours.'

'But I hate emptying the latrine bucket!' said Flavia. 'I hate it almost as much as I hate maths.'

'That's why it's a good punishment,' said Aristo mildly.

'A detective shouldn't have to empty latrine buckets.'

'For the last time: you are not a detective!'

'Yes I am!' Flavia's chair scraped on the marble floor as she stood up again. 'I'll prove it. Set me any mystery and I'll solve it for you. And . . . and if I can't do it I'll never mention the word "detective" again!'

'And you'll empty the latrine bucket every day for a month? Until the Saturnalia?'

'Yes,' said Flavia. 'But if I win, if I solve the mystery,' she continued, 'then we don't do

4

any maths for a whole month, we'll just read Greek myths.'

Aristo's brown eyes gleamed. 'Very well,' he said. 'Here's a mystery for you: why don't you find out who's been robbing Pistor the baker?'

Flavia's face fell. That was precisely the mystery she and her friends had been trying to solve for the past month. And it was proving to be a surprisingly difficult case.

'That's not a very important mystery,' she said airily. 'Isn't there a more exciting case we could solve? Like a murder? Or a kidnapping?'

'No,' said Aristo. 'I want you to find out who's been stealing Pistor's poppy-seed rolls. I'll give you three days. And today counts as the first.'

'Am I allowed to ask Jonathan and Nubia and Lupus to help me?' asked Flavia.

Aristo grinned up at her. 'Of course. I always encourage teamwork. If you'd conferred with the three of them yesterday you'd know how to do those calculations. But I'll bet you had your nose in a scroll, didn't you?'

Flavia nodded. 'I've been reading Ovid's *Metamorphoses*,' she murmured.

'What?' Aristo's face grew pale. 'You've been reading *what*?'

'Ovid's *Metamorphoses*?' said Flavia in a tiny voice.

'Where did you get it?'

Flavia tried to look innocent. 'From the top shelf in pater's study. Behind the Catullus,' she added.

'You know he put it out of reach because it's completely unsuitable for a young lady of your class.'

'But it's so good.'

'Of course it's good,' said Aristo. 'It's a masterpiece. But it's also extremely violent and full of unsuitable sex scenes. That's why Ovid was banned and exiled from Rome.'

'If I solve the mystery—' began Flavia.

'No!' cried Aristo.

'If I solve the mystery of who's stealing Pistor's bread,' Flavia persisted, 'then will you let us read bits of Ovid? Just the bits that aren't full of unsuitable sex and violence?'

'I suppose I could choose excerpts,' said Aristo slowly. He stood, too. 'Very well. If you solve that mystery in the next three days, we will read carefully selected passages from

6

Ovid instead of doing maths. But if you fail, then you'll empty the latrine bucket for a month, do your homework without a murmur, and never mention the word "detective" again. Agreed?'

'Agreed!' said Flavia.

And they shook on it.

'OK,' said Flavia Gemina to Jonathan, Nubia and Lupus. 'What do we know so far?'

The four friends and their three dogs were having a conference in Flavia's bedroom. The gongs and bells of Ostia had just finished clanging noon and through the bedroom door, they could hear the patter of a steady rain falling on the shrubs and trees of the inner garden.

Jonathan sat cross-legged on Nubia's bed next to his puppy, Tigris. 'Well,' he said, 'We know that the robberies have been going on for nearly half a year. Alma told us that.'

Flavia nodded. Her old nursemaid Alma was the cook in the Geminus household and did all the shopping. 'Alma told me that Pistor thinks it's an inside job,' she said.

'What is "inside job"?' asked Nubia. She had

learned Latin by listening to Virgil's *Aeneid*, and this was not an expression he used.

'It means the thief must be someone inside the bakery. One of Pistor's family, or one of his slaves. And you know what *that* means, don't you?' said Flavia.

They all looked at her.

'To solve an inside job,' said Flavia Gemina, 'we have to get inside!'

Jonathan liked Ostia's Imperial Granary. He liked the way it looked: red from the top of its terracotta roof-tiles to the bottom of its brick thresholds. And he loved the way it smelt of freshly-baked bread. That was because so many of Ostia's bakeries were situated around it.

Pistor's bakery was one of the smallest. But size didn't matter. Everyone knew Pistor's bread was the best: especially his poppy-seed rolls, which were even famous in Rome.

Jonathan's stomach rumbled as he caught the yeasty scent of hot bread. He followed his friend Lupus up the two steps to Pistor's shop front. It had stopped raining but the paving stones were still wet.

The boys pressed their faces against the damp wooden shutter. By putting his eye to one of the cracks between the horizontal slats, Jonathan could see the marble counter where bread was sold to the public between dawn and noon. Behind the counter was a doorway leading to the bakery beyond. A dim shape moved briefly in the doorway, then disappeared.

'Is there anyone in there?' said Flavia. 'I can smell fresh bread.'

'Yes,' said Jonathan. 'I can see them moving around.'

'I wonder if there's a back way in?' said Flavia.

'No,' said Jonathan, and pointed to a wooden door a few paces along. 'I think that's the only entrance.'

'Hark!' said Nubia. 'I am hearing a sound.'

They all listened and heard a faint donkey's bray. Jonathan frowned. 'It's coming from inside!'

'They are having a donkey inside the bakery?' said Nubia.

'I think,' said Flavia, 'that some bakeries use donkeys to grind the grain.'

'Why are you lot nosing around here?' said a voice behind them.

The four friends turned to find a pudgy boy standing on the rain-slicked street below them. He wore a long-sleeved tunic under a brown cloak and the sort of shoulder bag used by schoolboys to carry their wax tablets and scrolls. Jonathan guessed the boy was about his age: eleven or twelve.

'Can't you see we're closed?' said the boy, folding his arms across his chest.

'Hello,' said Flavia brightly. 'Do you work here?'

'*Work* here?' the boy snorted. 'Do I look like a slave? My father *owns* this bakery.'

'Oh. I'm sorry,' said Flavia, and then introduced herself. 'My name is Flavia Gemina, daughter of Marcus Flavius Geminus, sea captain. This is Jonathan, and Nubia and that's Lupus. Our tutor asked us to do a project on bread,' she lied. 'That's why we're looking around.'

'Bakeries close at noon, at the same time as the schools,' said the boy. 'Everybody knows that.'

'But we smelled bread,' said Jonathan.

'And we are hearing donkey,' added Nubia.

The boy looked at Nubia with interest and unfolded his arms. 'What did you say your name was?' he asked her.

'My name is Nubia.'

'I'm Sextus Nasenius Porcius,' said the boy. 'But you can call me Porcius. Everyone does.'

'Nice to meet you, Porcius,' said Flavia.

Porcius ignored her. 'I could give you a tour,' he said to Nubia. 'Would that help you with your project?'

'That would delight us,' said Nubia solemnly.

'Right,' said Porcius with a smile. 'Come on, then.'

Nubia looked around the first room of the bakery – a small storeroom filled with hemp sacks full of grain and flour. It was dim and warm. The low vaulted roof overhead and the pretty herringbone pattern of red bricks on the floor made it seem safe and cosy.

'The key to good bread,' Porcius told her, 'is good grain. We mainly use the finest Egyptian grain, from the Imperial Granary down the street. Come and see where we grind it.'

He led them into a spacious room with two big millstones and one smaller one, all made of dark-grey stone. To Nubia the millstones looked like stout women with tightly belted waists. Around each one circled a blindfolded donkey.

'Oh!' Nubia's hand went to her throat. 'The wretched creatures! Why do you blind them?'

'The blindfold doesn't hurt,' said Porcius. 'It's to stop them getting dizzy. They go round and round all day. See how they're yoked to the beam?' He led Nubia to the smallest millstone. The others followed.

A thin slave with hair the colour of dirty straw was pouring grain from a bag into the top of one of the millstones. He nodded respectfully at them.

Porcius ignored him. 'There's a gap between those two stones just wide enough to let the grain in. The donkey pulls the top stone around and the grain is crushed between the two stones and it comes out here as flour.' Porcius pointed to a trough.

But Nubia was not looking at the trough. She was looking at the place where years of donkeys' hooves had worn a smooth ring into the stone floor.

'Behold,' whispered Nubia. 'His fur is rubbing off his shoulders.'

'It doesn't hurt them much.' Porcius said. 'Animals don't feel pain like we do. Come on, I'll show you where we mix the flour with water to make the dough.'

Lupus followed the others into the next room. A big slave in a one-sleeved tunic stood at a marble trough. He was turning a vertical wooden bar. Lupus could see that the bar rotated blades which twisted the flour and water into an elastic dough.

As they approached, the slave looked up at them, and Lupus saw letters branded on his forehead: TENEME. Lupus knew that meant 'hold me' and that only slaves who kept trying to run away were branded on the forehead like this. The big slave gave Lupus a wink. His muscular chest and arms gleamed with sweat.

Lupus looked down into the marble trough. The mass of dough was smooth and slightly greyish.

'We bake our finest rolls first,' Porcius was

saying. 'Then in the late morning and early afternoon we bake ordinary bread – panis popularis – with the free grain that citizens receive. We only charge them for the cost of milling and baking. Hey!' Porcius looked around. 'Where's Nubia?'

Flavia spotted Nubia first: she was kneeling beside the smallest donkey. The slave with straw-coloured hair stood beside her. He had unharnessed the donkey and Nubia was stroking it.

'He is so little.' She looked up at them as they came in. 'Not even as big as Ferox.'

Flavia nodded. Ferox was her uncle's guard dog – a huge mastiff.

'You like animals?' said Porcius. 'Would you like to see my pets?'

Nubia's golden eyes lit up and she nodded.

'Come on then.' Porcius led them back through the store room and up a flight of dark stairs.

At the top of the stairs they met two women coming down. The first wore a light blue woollen stola with a dark blue palla draped over her head. Her face had been dusted with white powder to make it look fashionably pale. Behind her came a younger woman with frizzy brown hair and bad skin.

'Oh, hello, mater,' said Porcius. 'Are you going out?'

'Yes, dear,' said the powdered woman. 'Aren't you going to introduce me?'

'This is my mother, Fausta,' said Porcius. 'Mother, this is Nubia. And some friends of hers. I've been giving them a tour of the bakery.' He didn't bother to introduce the woman behind his mother and Flavia guessed that she must be a slave-girl.

'How nice,' said Fausta, patting his arm vaguely. She and her slave-girl continued past them. Flavia noticed that the slave-girl carried a bath-set: a bronze ring with strigil, tweezers, ear-scoop and oil-pot attached. From this clue she deduced that Porcius's mother and her slave-girl were going to the baths.

Flavia watched them out of sight, then turned and ran to catch up with the others.

'This is my room,' said Porcius. The pearly light of a November afternoon filled a long, narrow bedroom with a small balcony over-looking the road. 'And these are my steeds.'

Nubia uttered a cry of delight. On the table beside the bed was a delicate wooden cage. Nestled in the sawdust were several mice. Nubia counted at least six of them.

'And this,' Porcius gestured towards a big wooden box twice as long as his bed, 'is where they race.'

The box was open at the top and as Nubia looked down, she saw a wooden model of a racetrack. She recognised the layout because she had been to the Circus Maximus in Rome a few months earlier.

'I call it the Circus Minimus,' said Porcius, 'because it's the smallest racecourse in the world. 'Pater helped me build it.'

'You race your mice?' Jonathan raised an eyebrow.

'Yes,' said Porcius, setting the cage in the middle of the racetrack and opening the door. 'In two years, when I'm thirteen, I'm going to Rome to become a charioteer.'

'Do they have a school for that?' asked Jonathan.

Porcius shook his head. 'You have to join one of the faction stables and work your way up.'

'What are you doing?' came a female voice. 'Racing those silly mice again? You're so childish.'

Nubia and the others looked up. A girl of about fifteen stood in the doorway. She wore a sage-green tunic and had tied a lavender palla round her hips in a way Nubia knew was fashionable among young women in Rome. With her pale skin and dark wavy hair she would have been very pretty, if not for one flaw: she was cross-eyed.

'Who are *you*?' she asked, staring at Nubia and the others.

Flavia jumped to her feet. 'I'm Flavia Gemina, and these are my friends: Jonathan, Nubia and Lupus. You must be Titia.'

'I know you,' said Titia. 'You're Aristo's pupils.'

'That's right! Do you know him?'

Titia stood in the doorway for a moment without replying. Because of her cross-eyes, Nubia couldn't tell which of them she was looking at. Abruptly Titia moved away from the doorway and Nubia heard her footsteps retreating down the hallway.

'How rude!' muttered Flavia, sitting down again.

'Don't mind her,' said Porcius. He had brought out two tiny wooden chariots, each with a wooden rider fixed inside. 'She's always in a bad mood because she'll never find a husband.'

'Why not?' asked Nubia.

Porcius snorted. 'Didn't you see her? She's a cross-eyed freak. I think she's in love with your tutor, Aristo,' he added.

'How did you know that Aristo is our tutor?' asked Flavia.

'Everyone in Ostia knows. Or at least everybody at my school. They're all jealous because you have a private tutor who is nice to you and lets you do projects and doesn't beat you when you get a sum wrong.'

'What school do you go to?' asked Jonathan.

'The one in the forum,' said Porcius. 'But I don't want to talk about school. Let's have a chariot-race with mice!'

Ten minutes later, Flavia wiped tears of

laughter from her eyes. 'That was the funniest race I've ever seen. They're so cute. And so fast!'

'Yes,' said Porcius proudly as he scattered a handful of sunflower seeds onto the Circus Minimus, 'they're my boys.' The mice had been released from their tiny harnesses and they happily devoured their reward.

'Oh!' said Flavia suddenly. 'We're supposed to be solving – I mean studying – how bread is made.'

'Do you really want to go down to the boring old bakery again?' Porcius asked Nubia. She was holding one of the mice and stroking his tiny shoulder blades with her finger.

'Can you show us the ovens?' Flavia asked.

Porcius ignored Flavia. 'Nubia? he said. 'Do you want to go back down?'

'You can see the little donkey again,' Flavia said to Nubia.

Nubia's eyes lit up and she nodded firmly.

'Somebody whipped him!' cried Flavia.

The thin slave with straw-coloured hair was removing bread from a wall-oven. With his back turned to them, Flavia could see red welts on his neck and upper arms.

Porcius nodded. 'Pater beat the slaves yesterday to see if they knew anything about some missing bread rolls.' He noticed the look on Nubia's face. 'It doesn't hurt them much,' he said. 'Slaves don't feel pain like other people.'

Flavia heard Jonathan's stomach growl. 'Can we try some fresh rolls?' he asked. 'They smell delicious. I love warm bread.'

'No,' sighed Porcius. 'My father keeps strict account of every loaf of bread baked and sold. If a single roll goes missing he knows about it. He doesn't even let my mother take bread without asking. Oh, hello pater!' said Porcius, 'These are some friends of mine. They're studying how bread is made.'

A stocky man in a flour-dusted leather apron came through the doorway from the mill room. A tall boy of about thirteen trailed behind him.

'I know you,' said the short man to Flavia. He had onion breath. 'You're Alma's mistress.'

'That's right. I'm Flavia. These are my friends Nubia, Jonathan and Lupus.'

'Titus Nasenius Pistor. This is my eldest son Quintus, whom we call Ericius.'

The tall boy coughed and nodded a greeting. He was very thin with spiky hair and bluish shadows under his eyes.

'Hello,' said Flavia. 'We're studying how bread is made and Porcius has been showing us around.'

'That's my boy!' Pistor hooked his arm round Porcius's neck and gave his son an affectionate squeeze. 'He and Ericius here are going to take over the business one day.' Porcius squirmed free of his father's hairy arm, but Pistor didn't seem to mind. 'Any questions you'd like to ask me about the baking process?'

'How many slaves do you have here?' Flavia asked.

'Just the two,' said Pistor. 'The big one is Teneme and the one by the ovens is Romulus. He's also our accountant. This is a family business. Quality not quantity. The slaves do the milling and kneading and baking. I supervise. My family and I sell at the counter.'

Ericius coughed again, and Pistor slapped his tall son on the back. 'Both my boys do the early shift, before they go to school. Then my daughter Titia takes over.'

'Alma said some of your bread has been going missing,' said Flavia.

Pistor nodded. 'Been going on for months. At first the amount of disappearing bread was so small that I didn't notice. But I've been keeping strict accounts for the last few weeks and just this morning I calculated that it's almost always a dozen of my special poppy-seed rolls that go missing.'

'That's not very much,' said Jonathan.

Pistor scowled. 'It doesn't matter if it's one roll or a hundred. There's a thief in my household. That's what matters.' He spat onto the floor. 'But you know, it's very strange. The thefts only occur every seventh day. If the pattern continues, the thief will strike again soon.'

'Every seventh day,' said Flavia to the others as they walked back home. 'I know every eighth day we have the nundinae: the market days. But why every seventh day?'

'The Sabbath!' said Jonathan.

'Tomorrow's the Sabbath, isn't it?' said Flavia.

'Actually it starts this evening,' said Jonathan. 'You Romans start the day from sunrise. For us Jews, the day begins at sunset.'

'I'm glad you're Jewish,' said Flavia, 'and that Aristo lets us off lessons on the Sabbath, because that gives us an entire day to investigate. I think each one of us should follow a different member of Pistor's household tomorrow and see where they go! Agreed?'

They all nodded.

'Good,' said Flavia.

Early the next morning, just before dawn, the four friends stood watching Pistor's bakery from across the street. The bakery window was a glowing square of yellow where a line of hanging oil lamps illuminated Pistor and his two sons. They were already selling bread to a steady stream of customers.

Beyond them Flavia could see the slave called Romulus taking bread out of the ovens.

'Look at Pistor, chattering away like a magpie,' muttered Jonathan. 'His sons could eat a whole loaf and he wouldn't notice.'

Titus Nasenius Pistor was resting his fore-arms on the counter and gossiping with his customers. His two sons were doing most of the work, handing out bread and taking coins.

Flavia's door-slave Caudex and her old nurse Alma were among those in the queue. This was their daily routine.

Flavia had rarely been out of the house this early and she was surprised to see how busy Ostia was before dawn. It was chilly and she could smell the smoke from the torches people held.

She shivered and pulled her woollen palla tighter round her shoulders. Her bare legs were cold, too, so she stood closer to Scuto's warm bulk. He looked up at her, and gave his tail a tentative wag as if to say, *Can we go now?* Flavia shook her head at him, so he sighed and sat down on the pavement.

Presently Alma stood silhouetted in front of the bright rectangle above the bakery counter. She chatted with Pistor for a few minutes, then followed torch-bearing Caudex across the street to where Flavia stood with her friends.

Alma smiled and handed out bread rolls. 'There you go, my dears,' she said. 'Try those.'

'Behold!' said Nubia. 'They are warm.'

Jonathan bit into his. 'And delicious!'

Flavia tore off a chunk of her warm roll for Scuto, who was on his feet again. He devoured it in one gulp and kept his eyes fixed on her face.

Lupus chomped his roll carefully with his molars, then tipped his head back to swallow. He had no tongue and every bite of food threatened to choke him.

Jonathan grinned. 'Got any more of those?' he asked Alma.

Lupus pointed at Jonathan's mouth and laughed.

'Ewww, Jonathan!' cried Flavia. 'You've got lots of little black seeds stuck between your teeth.'

'Poppy-seeds,' said Alma, and fished in her coin-purse. 'Do you want to borrow my tooth-pick, Jonathan?'

'I have one,' said Jonathan, reaching into his own belt-pouch. 'Made of ivory. Birthday present from my aunt,' he explained as he began to pick his teeth. 'Hey!' He cried. 'I have an idea. We could tell jokes to everyone in Pistor's house and when they laugh we can look at the their teeth and see who's been eating poppy-seed rolls.'

Lupus guffawed but Flavia merely gave Jonathan a look.

'Do you want to come with us now, dears?' asked Alma. 'Caudex and I usually go to the meat-market next.'

'You carry on shopping, Alma,' said Flavia. 'But can we borrow Caudex?'

The sky was pale in the east when two dark shapes emerged from the door of the bakery and moved off in the direction of the forum.

'There go the boys,' whispered Flavia. 'After them, Lupus!'

Lupus grinned; he loved following people. Crouching low, he ran after Porcius and Ericius.

A loud rattling noise behind Flavia made her start in alarm. She turned to see a sleepy-looking man in a grey tunic and she breathed a sigh of relief: it was only the owner of the thermopolium pulling up his shutter.

'You waiting for me to open?' he yawned. 'Have a seat and I'll be with you in a moment.'

'We may as well,' whispered Flavia to the

others. 'If we sit here and have a cup of hot spiced wine, we'll be less conspicuous.'

'Behold,' said Nubia, as they sat on wooden stools beside a low marble-topped bar. 'Pistor's wife and daughter are now serving bread.'

'But he's still busy chatting to his friends,' snorted Flavia.

There was no longer a queue outside the bakery, but a steady trickle of customers came and went.

Flavia and her friends had drunk a beaker of hot spiced wine – well-watered – when Titia disappeared from the bakery counter. A few moments later the bakery door opened and she appeared, her palla draped modestly over her head.

'There goes Titia!' said Flavia with satisfaction. 'Nubia, you and Caudex follow her. And don't let her spot you. She knows who you are.'

By mid-morning Jonathan's stomach was growling loudly. He had only eaten one bread roll and drunk some weak spiced wine. He and Flavia had moved away from the bar to sit at a wooden table of the thermopolium. They both warmed their feet beneath Scuto's furry stomach.

'I'm hungry,' Jonathan remarked. 'It seems like I'm always hungry these days.'

'Here.' Flavia grinned at him and pushed a silver coin across the table. 'Buy a couple of their rolls. We'll see how good they are.'

'Not as good as Pistor's,' said Jonathan a moment later. He handed Flavia a roll and took a bite of his own. 'Ow!' He reached into his mouth and pulled something out.

'What is it?' asked Flavia, alarmed.

'Bit of grit. I could have broken a tooth. No,' he said, 'these rolls are definitely not up to Pistor's standards.'

An hour later Flavia sighed deeply. 'I wish I had a scroll to read. It's boring just sitting here watching the bakery doorway.'

'Shall I teach you that prayer we say every morning? You told me you wanted to learn it.'

'The one about daily bread?' said Flavia. 'Yes, please!'

'It starts like this,' said Jonathan, 'Pater noster, our father . . .'

'Pater noster,' repeated Flavia, and then she gasped and pointed. 'There goes the runaway slave!'

'What?'

'Teneme. And look how fast he's moving! Quick, Jonathan. Follow him!'

'Good morning, sir,' said Flavia casually, and leaned on the cold marble counter of the bakery. 'May I have one of your famous poppy-seed rolls?'

'Of course,' said Pistor. 'That will be one dupondius.'

Flavia put down a brass coin, accepted the roll and took a bite.

'Still working on your project?' he asked.

Flavia's mouth was full, so she nodded.

'Then why don't you come on in?'

Flavia swallowed. 'May my dog come in, too?'

Pistor nodded and jerked his head towards the door. 'It's open.'

A moment later, Flavia and Scuto entered

the bakery. As usual, it was warm and fragrant with the smell of fresh bread. Apart from Pistor, there was only a slave sitting at a table in a corner.

Pistor had just turned to serve a customer, so Flavia wandered over to the table. Scuto followed her, his toenails tapping on the brick floor. He sniffed the slave's knees and wagged his tail.

The fair-haired slave stopped flicking beads on his abacus and reached down to scratch Scuto behind the ear.

'You're Romulus, aren't you?' said Flavia to the slave.

He nodded.

Flavia casually ran her finger over some letters etched into the wooden surface of his small table. 'Do you keep the accounts?'

'Yes,' sighed Romulus, picking up his quill and making a note on a piece of papyrus. 'The master likes to account for every loaf and roll. I even have to note how many are burnt in the ovens.'

Flavia nodded, then frowned. 'What's this?' she said, pointing to the inscription in the table.

Romulus flushed. 'Oh, that. It's just a game. A puzzle.'

Flavia turned her head. 'What does it say? The sower . . . holds . . . the works?'

```
S A T O R
A R E P O
T E N E T
O P E R A
R O T A S
```

'It says, "The sower, Arepo, holds the wheels at work".'

'It's not very good Latin,' said Flavia with a frown. 'What does it mean?'

'It doesn't really mean anything. But if you write it out . . .' He opened a wax tablet, turned it sideways and wrote in tiny neat letters:

SATORAREPOTENETOPERAROTAS

'It reads the same backwards as it does forwards,' said Romulus.

'Oh!' Flavia hopped with excitement. 'I

know those kinds of codes. They have a special name. It's called a . . . a . . .'

'Palindrome,' said Romulus.

'Yes!' cried Flavia. '*Palin* means "back" in Greek and *drome* means "runs". A palindrome is a word that runs the same way backwards as it does forwards.'

'And there are other ways you can play with it, too,' said Romulus.

'You're very educated for a bakery-slave,' said Flavia suddenly.

Romulus nodded sadly. 'I used to be a schoolteacher until I fell into debt and had to sell myself into slavery.'

'Did you ever teach Pistor's sons?' asked Flavia.

'No,' said Romulus. 'Though I'd like to. Pelops and Erysichthon are bright boys.'

'Who?'

'Oh, those are just my private nicknames for Porcius and Ericius. No,' sighed Romulus. 'I was never a private tutor. Before they let me go, I used to be schoolmaster at the Forum School.'

★

I'M GLAD I DON'T GO TO THE FORUM SCHOOL wrote Lupus on his wax tablet.

'Why not?' asked Flavia, taking a cube of white goats' cheese. It was noon and they were having a light lunch of cheese and olives back at her house.

Lupus took his brass stylus in his right hand and pretended to bring it down hard on the knuckles of his left.

'They beat you?' asked Jonathan.

Lupus nodded. Then he twisted his own ear and grimaced.

'And they twist your ear?' asked Flavia.

Lupus nodded again and wrote on his tablet:

THEY RECITE EVERYTHING
SO BORING he added.

'Did Porcius or Ericius pull any bread rolls out of their shoulder bags?' asked Flavia. 'Maybe to sell them to their classmates? Or bribe the master not to beat them?'

Lupus shook his head and wrote on the tablet: NO ROLLS

'So that probably rules out those two,' murmured Flavia. 'What about you, Nubia?

Titia didn't notice that you were following her, did she?'

'No,' said Nubia. 'I and Caudex are very hidden. We follow her to market and then to temple of Venus. Caudex waits outside and I pull palla over my head and go in her behind.'

Lupus gave Nubia his bug-eyed look.

'You mean you went in behind her,' said Jonathan, and grinned at Lupus.

'Yes. Titia gives the lady priest a coin and puts clay eyes on the shrine.'

'A model of eyes, made of clay?' said Flavia. Nubia nodded.

'That will be a votive,' said Flavia. 'A votive is a model of the part of your body you want cured. It reminds the goddess of your prayer. She probably wants her eyes healed.'

'Is there something wrong with somebody's eyes?' said Alma, coming into the dining room. She set a platter of poppy-seed rolls on the table.

They all reached for one and Flavia nodded. 'Pistor's daughter Titia. She has cross eyes and wants to be beautiful to win a husband.'

'Oh yes, Titia. The poor thing,' said Alma. 'Pomegranate juice or barley water?'

'Pomegranate juice, please.' As Alma went out Flavia turned to Jonathan.

'You followed Teneme. Did he run away again?'

'No.' Jonathan sighed and spat an olive stone onto his plate. 'Teneme just went to the Imperial Granary and stood in a queue and collected a big bag of grain. Then he brought it back to the bakery. He arrived just as you left, Flavia. I saw you and Scuto walking home. Did you find out anything?'

'Not really. I talked to the slave called Romulus. He does the accounts. Apparently Pistor keeps track of every roll they sell. But there was one thing . . . It might even be a clue.'

'What?'

'Romulus is very educated. In fact, he used to be a teacher at the Forum School. He collects puzzles and codes like me, and he's given Porcius and Ericius private nicknames. He calls Porcius Pelops, which makes sense.'

'Pelops?' asked Jonathan. 'Who's Pelops?'

'He was a character from Greek mythology who loved racing chariots,' said Flavia. 'And we know Porcius is mad for the races, so that fits. But Romulus called Ericius something else. Eris-eek-something.' She chewed an olive thoughtfully. 'Erysichthon. That's it! Now if only I could remember where I've seen that name . . .'

Alma came into the dining room with four beakers on a tray.

'You know,' said Jonathan, 'There are still two people we haven't followed.'

Flavia nodded. 'Pistor's wife Fausta,' she said, 'and her slave-girl.'

'Oh my dears, you don't want to follow Fausta,' said Alma, setting down the tray and handing out the beakers.

'Why not?' said Flavia, taking a sip of pomegranate juice.

'She's far too preoccupied to steal her own bread,' said Alma, and then lowered her voice to a scandalised whisper. 'It's common knowledge that she and her slave-girl spend all their time down at the Forum Baths, watching the gladiators exercise!'

Flavia sneezed as she opened the dusty lid of the leather scroll-case. She had brought it down from the top shelf of her father's tablinum.

Nubia looked round nervously. 'Flavia. You are not supposed to be reading the Ovid.'

'I know. That's why the boys are keeping a lookout for pater.' She glanced over at Jonathan and Lupus, standing in the wide doorway of the study. 'Any sign of him?'

They shook their heads.

Flavia nodded with satisfaction and turned back to the scroll case. 'Eight. I think it's in scroll eight.' Her finger hovered over the open case for a moment. Finally she pulled out a scroll and unrolled it on her father's desk. Nubia watched Flavia expertly twist her hands so that the blocks of writing scrolled past her eyes.

At last Flavia whispered: '*Eureka!* A king named Erysichthon scorned the gods and they cursed him with a hunger so terrible that he devoured his own flesh!'

Nubia stared at Flavia in horror. 'That is a story of Ovid?'

Flavia nodded as she rolled up the scroll and dropped it back into its cylindrical case.

'I'll bet Romulus calls Ericius "Erysichthon"

because he's always hungry.' She climbed up onto her father's cedarwood table and replaced the scroll case on the highest shelf.

'Jonathan,' she said, as she jumped down off the table again.

'Yes?'

'Do you think your father would mind if I asked him a medical question?'

'Worms,' said Jonathan's father, Doctor Mordecai ben Ezra. He had heavy-lidded eyes, a sharp nose and an accent. 'Roundworms, tapeworms, whipworms. They are all types of parasite, which can make a man ravenously hungry. Other symptoms include coughing, wheezing and vomiting.'

'Yes!' cried Flavia. 'Ericius coughed a lot. And he doesn't look very well.'

'What is parasite?' asked Nubia.

'It's an animal that lives off another animal to survive,' said Mordecai. 'Sometimes they live inside us.'

The girls looked at one another and shuddered.

'Ugh,' said Flavia. 'I could never be a doctor.'

'Why not?' Mordecai smiled at her from beneath his dark turban. 'Doctors solve mysteries, too. We have to discover the underlying causes for things that happen.'

'I think I have worms,' said Jonathan. 'I wheeze.'

'That's because you have asthma,' said Mordecai. 'I'm fairly certain you don't have worms.'

'But I'm hungry all the time.'

'And that's because you're an eleven-year-old boy. Your body is growing faster now than at almost any time in your life. It needs bread to live.'

'But how can I tell whether I have worms?'

'After you've been to the latrine, you must take the bucket into bright sunlight and carefully examine your stool.'

'My stool?' Jonathan looked puzzled. Then understanding dawned in his eyes: 'My stool! Ugh!'

Lupus guffawed.

'Yes,' said Jonathan's father. 'And if you see anything . . . er . . . moving there, then you probably have worms.'

Flavia looked at Mordecai. 'So if I wanted to

find out whether Ericius has worms, then I'd have to . . .'

Mordecai nodded. 'You'd have to take his latrine bucket and have a good look.'

Flavia looked ruefully at her three friends. 'I guess,' she said, 'a detective *does* have to empty latrine buckets after all.'

'You were absolutely right,' said Mordecai, coming into Flavia's atrium a few hours later. 'I've just been round to Pistor's. I'm afraid young Ericius does have worms. I've prescribed a tincture of pomegranate skins and wormwood, after a three day purge. Poor boy.'

'I guess you can't blame him for stealing the bread rolls,' said Flavia. 'I just hope his father doesn't beat him.'

'Oh, he's not your culprit,' said Mordecai. 'I spoke to him gently and he swore he wasn't the thief.'

'And you believed him?' said Jonathan.

'Yes. The poor boy lives in fear of his father.'

'Pollux!' muttered Flavia. 'If Ericius didn't steal the bread rolls, then who did?'

'Let me have your theories,' said Flavia, after Jonathan's father had left. She absently scratched a flea-bite on her big toe. 'And remember to give me the motive, means and method. That's what Admiral Pliny wrote in his scroll.'

They were sitting in her bedroom, the girls on Flavia's bed, the boys on Nubia's.

Jonathan cleared his throat. 'My theory is that Porcius is stealing the rolls,' he said. 'His motive could be to sell them in order to raise money so that he can run away to join a racing faction in Rome. His father obviously wants him to become a baker, not a charioteer.'

'That's an excellent motive,' said Flavia. 'And we know he has the means; he works at the shopfront every morning. But what about his method?'

'I'm not sure,' said Jonathan. 'Maybe he slips some rolls into his shoulder bag and then sells them to the other boys in his class.'

'But you didn't see him take any rolls from his bag. And remember, it was always a dozen rolls and it's only every seven days.'

Jonathan sighed. 'I know. That's what I can't figure out.'

'You have to take every clue into account when you're solving a mystery,' said Flavia. 'Nubia, who do you think stole the bread?'

'I think Titia is stealing poppy-seed rolls for Venus, goddess of love. Titia does this so that Venus will be favourable to her prayers and uncross her eyes so she can marry a fine man.'

'Good reasoning,' said Flavia. 'But again: why a dozen rolls, and why every seven days?'

Suddenly Lupus gave a grunt of excitement.

I KNOW WHY XII he wrote on his tablet.

They all leaned forward eagerly as he wrote: EACH TRAY FOR ROLLS HOLDS XII

'Brilliant!' cried Flavia. 'Someone could grab a tray and take it, rolls and all. But have any trays been stolen?'

'The thief doesn't have to steal the tray,' said Jonathan. 'He could just grab the tray, quickly empty it into a sack or shoulder bag, then put it back.'

'And maybe the person's bag holds just about twelve rolls,' continued Flavia. She sighed. 'That doesn't really help us. Titia could put twelve rolls in her shopping basket but the boys' school shoulder bags could hold about a dozen rolls, too.'

Lupus wrote on his tablet: I THINK TENEME DID IT

'Motive, means and method,' said Flavia briskly. 'What motive would he have? Why would he steal bread rolls?'

SUPPLIES FOR IF HE RUNS AWAY AGAIN?

'That's worth considering. But remember, the thefts have been occurring for half a year. If he's been storing up supplies for when he runs away . . . Well, some of those rolls will be very stale.' Flavia sucked a strand of hair which had come unpinned. 'And we still come back to that strange clue: why every seven days? I'm certain that's the key to this mystery.'

'Tomorrow,' said Flavia. 'I'd like to post watch on Pistor's bakery again. We'll have to do it before lessons, so we'll need to be up very early.' Flavia tore a piece from the last of the special plaited Sabbath loaf. She and Nubia had been invited to eat dinner at Jonathan's and now the four friends were dining with his sister Miriam and his father Mordecai. The six of them sat on floor cushions around a low hexagonal table.

'Tomorrow early?' said Jonathan, with a glance at his father. 'I can't tomorrow.'

'Why not? The Sabbath is over, isn't it?'

'You know why not,' said Jonathan and Lupus gave her his bug-eyed look as if to say, 'Well?'

'No, I don't.'

'Flavia,' said Mordecai. 'Tomorrow Jonathan and Miriam and Lupus and I will be celebrating the Lord's supper, as we do on the first day of every week. You know that Rome frowns on our faith. That's why we have to meet very early, and in secret.'

'I'm sorry,' said Flavia. 'I forgot you're Christians as well as Jews.' She sighed. 'Then I guess it's just you and me, Nubia.'

That night Flavia couldn't sleep.

She kept thinking of all the mysteries she had solved in her short career as a detective. She thought about the assassin they had exposed in Rome: how his disguise had almost tricked them. She thought about the kidnappers from Pompeii: how the obvious culprit was innocent. She thought about the blacksmith's riddle: how it had turned out to be a secret coded password.

Flavia opened her eyes, rolled over onto her stomach and took the wax tablet she always kept beside her bed. The dimly burning night oil-lamp gave her just enough light to see as she wrote on it. She etched the words of Romulus's magic square into the yellow beeswax and noticed that the word TENET appeared as a cross in the centre, and that there was a pleasing symmetry of letters.

```
S A T O R
A R E P O
T E N E T
O P E R A
R O T A S
```

She looked at it for a while, then used the flat end of her stylus to rub it out and rewrite the letters as a palindrome, the sentence which could be read both backwards and forwards. 'The sower, Arepo, holds the wheels at work.'

'What a strange sentence,' she murmured to herself.

Then a thought occurred to her. Maybe it was written in Caesar's Code. Aristo had told them about a cypher invented by the great commander Julius Caesar. In his coded messages, every letter represented a letter three places further on in the Latin alphabet.

Underneath the palindrome she wrote the letters three places on:

S A T O R A R E P O T E N E T O P E R A R O T A S
X D Z R V D V H S R Z H P H Z R S H V D V R Z D X

'That makes no sense!' she murmured. 'Not that *The sower, Arepo, holds the wheels at work* makes much sense . . .'

She tried other sequences using letters earlier or later in the alphabet, and she even tried substituting characters from the Greek alphabet, but she could see that they were all gibberish. Finally, Flavia sighed and yawned and put down the wax tablet and lay back on her bed.

She closed her eyes. And smiled. She could still see the letters, like black ants, running back and forth across the creamy parchment of her mind. Her body felt heavy and warm; she knew she was drifting into sleep. The letters were moving, slowly rearranging themselves to form patterns. A circle. A diamond. A cross . . .

Suddenly Flavia was wide awake. She opened her eyes, lifted herself on one elbow and picked up the wax tablet again. One type of code she hadn't thought to try was an anagram, where the letters are rearranged to form new words.

Presently she uttered a small cry of triumph.

At the foot of her bed, Scuto lifted his big head and thumped his tail.

'I've cracked the code, Scuto!' she whispered. 'And I think I've solved the mystery, too!'

Nubia did not understand why she and Flavia had got up in the middle of the night or why they now stood shivering by the shuttered thermopolium, watching the door of Pistor's bakery for the third time in as many days. It was so early that the bakery window was not even open yet.

Low in the west, a full moon cast an eerie wash of silver over the deserted streets of Ostia.

'I do not think we should be out at night alone,' said Nubia in a small voice.

'You're absolutely right,' agreed Flavia in a whisper. 'We could get kidnapped or murdered. Look! The bakery door is opening!' She quickly pinched out the flame of her small clay oil-lamp.

Someone moved out of the inky shadows. It was a figure in a hooded cape, holding a flickering oil-lamp. From this distance Nubia could not tell if it was a man or a woman. But she could clearly see the bulging bag slung over one shoulder. As they watched, the hooded figure turned towards Ostia's main road, the Decumanus Maximus.

'Come on, Nubia,' hissed Flavia.

They slipped out of their protective shadow and moved quietly after the figure, staying on the pavement close to the shuttered shops. Somewhere in the distance a dog barked, but their felt boots made no sound on the cold paving stones and the girls did not alert any watchdogs nearby.

Presently the hooded figure knocked softly on the double doors of the Imperial Granary. The door opened immediately and there was a whispered greeting. The figure disappeared inside and the door closed.

'Pollux!' cursed Flavia under her breath.

'Behold!' Nubia pointed. 'Other persons is coming.'

The two girls pressed themselves into the inky shadows of a doorway and watched two women move quickly across the narrow street. From the ragged pallas which covered their heads Nubia could tell they were poor, perhaps even slaves.

Then a man arrived from the direction of the theatre. The silver moonlight illuminated him, too, and before he slipped inside, Nubia saw that he wore the conical hat of a freedman. Next to arrive were a man and woman with three little girls: an entire family! The father whispered something – presumably a password – and they disappeared inside. Then all was silent.

'Come on,' whispered Flavia after several minutes. 'Let's go closer.'

The brick walls of the granary were thick

enough to keep out fire and damp, and the double wooden doors were heavy, too, but as they stood outside, Nubia could distinctly hear the faint sound of singing.

The moon sank behind the town wall to the west and plunged Ostia into darkness. Flavia wished they had a light, but she had pinched out the flame of her oil-lamp and she had no sulphur sticks to re-light it. On the other side of the double wooden doors, the singing had given way to chanting.

'You girls shouldn't be out alone,' said a deep voice right behind Flavia.

The girls started in terror.

The man laughed and stretched out his arm to reach past them and knock on the door. 'Come in out of the cold,' he said to them, and to the person who opened the door a few moments later: 'The sower, Arepo, holds the wheels at work.'

'Welcome, brother Stephanos,' said the doorkeeper. 'Er . . . and sisters.'

Flavia was swept inside with Nubia. She caught a glimpse of a vast, dim, columned court-yard flickering in the light of a few torches.

Then the man guided them towards a room on the left.

He pushed open another wooden door and they stepped into a small storeroom, bare apart from a few sacks of grain and warmed by a brazier in its centre. As they entered, a dozen lamplit faces turned to look at them. Most of the faces relaxed into smiles of welcome and curiosity, but one face grew pale.

It was the face of the thief.

'How did you know it was me?' asked Romulus, as the three of them walked back towards the bakery. The fair-haired slave was holding a sack from the granary, his pretext for being out of the house.

'Your secret code was the clue I needed.' Flavia opened her wax tablet and held her clay oil-lamp up to it. 'It's a magic square and a palindrome, but it's also an anagram. If you rearrange the letters and put them in the shape of a cross, you can spell out PATER NOSTER twice, once vertically and once horizontally, with two As and two Os left over. Alpha and omega: the first and last letters of the Greek alphabet. *I am the Alpha and the Omega, the Beginning and the End.'*

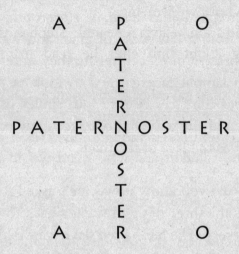

'How do you know about alpha and omega?' said Romulus. 'Do you follow The Way?'

'No, but my friend Jonathan does. They have secret meetings, too.'

'Ah! The doctor's son. They're the Jewish believers.'

'Yes,' said Flavia. 'Jonathan has been teaching me your prayer. The one about our father in heaven giving us bread and forgiving us.'

She looked at Romulus. 'Is Arepo another name for your god?'

He nodded. 'It's a secret name for God's son, whom we worship.'

'God's son,' Flavia repeated. 'Stephanos was talking about him after he read from the scroll.'

Romulus gave her a shy glance. 'Did you like it? Our service, I mean?'

'Yes,' said Flavia thoughtfully. 'Yes, I did. I still don't understand why a god would sacrifice his own son for us. But the room had a nice feeling. And everybody seemed so happy, even though they were poor.'

'And do you see now why I take the bread? Did you see those little girls' eyes light up when we celebrated the Lord's supper and they each received one of Pistor's finest poppy-seed rolls?'

Flavia nodded, then stopped in the street. Nubia and Romulus stopped, too.

'But Romulus—'

'I know,' he said. 'I've been stealing and it's wrong. The moment I saw you come in I felt bad. I knew God was disappointed in me. I suppose I've been justifying my theft: "Do not muzzle an ox while it is treading out the grain." '

'What?'

'Nothing.' He shook his head. 'You know, some masters give their slaves a few coins, or the odd gift. Pistor doesn't give us anything. Only the lash. But I won't steal the rolls again. I promise.'

'Good,' said Flavia.

'You won't give me away, will you? My master could sell me to the mines. Or have me crucified. I swear it will never happen again.'

Flavia looked at Nubia, who knew the truth. Jonathan and Lupus would have to be told, too.

But nobody else could know. Not even Aristo.

Flavia sighed at the thought of emptying the latrine bucket for a month and of doing maths instead of reading Ovid. She thought of how smug Aristo would be when she admitted defeat.

But really it didn't matter, because now she knew for certain that she was a detective. And that she had a gift for finding the truth.

In the dark streets of Ostia, holding her little clay oil-lamp, Flavia Gemina looked up at the slave who stood before her.

'No, Romulus,' she said with a smile. 'I promise I won't breathe a word.'

FINIS

ARISTO'S SCROLL

abacus (*ab*-ak-uss)
   from Greek *abakos* ('slab') an ancient calculator
   using beads on wires

atrium (*eh*-tree-um)
   the reception room in larger Roman homes,
   often with skylight and pool

Catullus (kat-*ull*-uss)
   Gaius Valerius Catullus (died 54 BC); Latin
   poet famous for his saucy love poetry

Circus Maximus (*sir*-kuss *max*-im-uss)
   greatest racecourse in the Roman world; its
   remains can still be seen in Rome

Decumanus   Maximus   (dek-you-*man*-uss
max-ee-muss)
   main road of many Roman cities, named after
   the gate of the original fort

detectrix (day-*tek*-tricks)
   feminine form of 'detector': someone who
   uncovers or reveals something

domina (*dom*-in-ah)

    Latin word which means 'mistress'; a polite
form of address for a woman

dupondius (doo-*pon*-dee-uss)

    a brass coin worth perhaps 50p in today's
money (half a sestertius)

Erysichthon (eris-*eek*-thon)

    according to Ovid's *Metamorphoses* book VIII,
this king chopped down a sacred tree and was
punished by Demeter with an all-consuming
hunger

Etruscan (ee-*truss*-kan)

    language (and people) from Etruria, an area of
Italy north of Rome

Flavia (*flay*-vee-a)

    a name, meaning 'fair-haired'; Flavius is the
masculine form of this name

forum (*for*-um)

    ancient marketplace and civic centre in Roman
towns

gladiator

    man trained to fight other men in the arena,
sometimes to the death

Italia (it-*al*-ya)

    the Latin word for Italy

Metamorphoses (met-uh-*morf*-oh-seez)
  see Ovid (below)

Minerva (min-*erv*-uh)
  Roman equivalent of Athena, the Greek
  goddess of wisdom and war

nundinae (*noon*-din-eye)
  Latin for 'market days'

Ostia (*oss*-tee-uh)
  port about 16 miles southwest of Rome; Ostia
  is Flavia's home town

Ovid (*ov*-id)
  Publius Ovidius Naso (died AD 17); Roman
  poet banned by Augustus; his masterpiece
  is the *Metamorphoses*, poems about mythic
  transformations

pater (*pah*-tare)
  Latin for 'father'

palla (*pal*-uh)
  a woman's cloak, could also be wrapped round
  the waist or worn over the head

panis popularis (*pan*-iss pop-you-*lar*-iss)
  bread made from the free ration of grain
  allotted to every Roman citizen

papyrus (puh-*pie*-russ)
  papery material made of pounded Egyptian

reeds, used as writing paper and also for
parasols and fans

Pelops (*pee*-lops)
man from Greek mythology who won his wife
by cheating at a chariot race

peristyle (*perry*-style)
a columned walkway around an inner garden
or courtyard

Pollux (*pol*-luks)
one of the famous twins of Greek mythology
(Castor being the other)

scroll (skrole)
papyrus or parchment 'book', unrolled from
side to side as it was read

stola (stole-uh)
long tunic usually worn by Roman matrons
(married women)

strigil (*strij*-ill)
blunt-edged, curved tool for scraping off dead
skin, oil and dirt at the baths

stylus (*stile*-us)
metal, wood or ivory tool for writing on wax
tablets

tablinum (tab-*leen*-um)
room in wealthier Roman houses used as the

master's study or office, often looking out onto
the atrium or inner garden, or both

thermopolium (therm-oh-*pole*-ee-um)
a restaurant or bar, which serves warm drinks
and snacks

Titus (*tie*-tuss)
Titus Flavius Vespasianus, forty-year-old son
of Vespasian, has been Emperor of Rome for
about half a year when this story takes place

tunic (*tew*-nic)
piece of clothing like a big T-shirt; children
often wore a long-sleeved one

Virgil (*vur*-jill)
Publius Vergilius Maro (died 19 BC); Latin poet
who, among other things, wrote a famous epic
poem called the *Aeneid*

wax tablet
wax-covered rectangular piece of wood used
for making notes

Read more Roman Mysteries!

I THE THIEVES OF OSTIA

Together, the four Roman friends work out who severed the heads of the watchdogs that guard people's homes, and the motive behind the crimes . . .

II THE SECRETS OF VESUVIUS

The four friends travel to Pompeii to solve a riddle that may lead to treasure, but then tragedy strikes – Mount Vesuvius erupts and the children are fleeing for their lives, in one of the worst natural disasters ever recorded.

III THE PIRATES OF POMPEII

Following the eruption of Mount Vesuvius, Flavia and her friends discover that children are being kidnapped from the refugee camps along the Bay of Naples, and together they solve the mystery of the pirates of Pompeii.

IV THE ASSASSINS OF ROME

The four friends travel to Rome on a dangerous mission, where they inadvertently discover the terrible truth about Jonathan's family history . . .

V THE DOLPHINS OF LAURENTUM

After Flavia learns, to her horror, that her family is in danger of losing everything they own, events take the friends to an opulent seaside villa. There they discover a sunken treasure, and unwittingly solve the terrible mystery of Lupus's past.

VI THE TWELVE TASKS OF FLAVIA GEMINA

The festival of Saturnalia leads to some wild behaviour, when a Roman widow shows a little too much interest in Flavia's father! To unearth this woman's motives, Flavia must perform twelve tasks, just like the Greek hero Hercules.

VII THE ENEMIES OF JUPITER

The fever which started in Ostia is now threatening to become a plague in Rome. The young detectives must use all their skills to solve a dangerous mystery for the Emperor Titus.

VIII THE GLADIATORS FROM CAPUA

In Rome, a search for the missing Jonathan, leads the detectives straight to the inaugural games – plus wild beasts, criminals, conspirators and gladiators.

IX THE COLOSSUS OF RHODES

The friends sail to the island of Rhodes, site of one of the seven wonders of the ancient world . . . and base of a criminal mastermind!

X THE FUGITIVE FROM CORINTH

Flavia and her three friends set off for Delphi in pursuit of their tutor, Aristo . . .

XI THE SIRENS OF SURRENTUM

Passions run deep beneath the tranquil surface in a summer holiday adventure . . . Can Flavia and her friends track down the would-be poisoner at the Villa Limona?

XII THE CHARIOTEER OF DELPHI

In Rome the detectives find themselves embroiled in a campaign to sabotage one of the rival racing factions. Can they catch the culprit in time?

Also look out for:

THE FIRST ROMAN MYSTERIES QUIZ BOOK (March 2007)

Test your knowledge of the characters, places and events in the series with these fun and fiendish questions.

This quiz book features questions about the characters, places and events occurring in books I–VI of the Roman Mysteries. In addition, there will be pictorial questions, quizzes about ancient Roman food, fashion, customs and history.

ROMAN MYSTERIES MINI-MYSTERIES (June 2007)

Find out what else has been going on between each exciting instalment of the Roman Mysteries series . . .

THE SECOND ROMAN MYSTERIES QUIZ BOOK
(July 2007)

This quiz book features questions about the characters, places and events occurring in books VII–XII of the Roman Mysteries. In addition, there will be pictorial questions, quizzes about ancient Roman transport, fashion, customs and history. Plus there will be philosophical conundrums, brainteasers and Roman riddles. Answers supplied at the back of the book.